Two Friends

Susan B. Anthony and Frederick Douglass

BY

Dean Robbins

ILLUSTRATED BY

Sean Qualls

& Selina Alko

ORCHARD BOOKS • AN IMPRINT OF SCHOLASTIC INC. • NEW YORK

We gratefully acknowledge Mary Huth from the

National Susan B. Anthony Museum & House for her astute,

generous, and meticulous fact-checking of the text.

Library of Congress Cataloging-in-Publication Data Available

ISBN 978-0-545-39996-8

10 9 8 7 6 5 4 3 2 1   16 17 18 19 20

Printed in Malaysia   108
First edition, January 2016

A Note from Sean and Selina

In making the art for *Two Friends*, we began by researching the time period when Susan B. Anthony and Frederick Douglass met for tea, as well as their separate histories leading up to that afternoon. We read books and looked at many photographs and depictions of the clothing typically worn at the time. We drew several rounds of sketches to get the setting and tone of the story just right. Then, using acrylic paint, collage, and colored pencil, we created mixed-media spreads, finishing off each other's visual sentences whenever necessary. In the end, we feel we achieved something entirely new—an integration of our styles, a true collaboration.

The illustrations were created using mixed media: paint (gouache and acrylic), collage, and colored pencil on bristol board.

The text type was set in Hoefler Text Roman, Hoefler Bold Small Caps, and Hoefler Italic Swash. The display type was set in Hoefler Black Italic Swash.

On page 32: Photo of Susan B. Anthony courtesy of the National Susan B. Anthony Museum & House, Rochester, NY, susanbanthonyhouse.org • Photo of Frederick Douglass from the collection of the Onondaga Historical Association, 321 Montgomery Street, Syracuse, NY 13202

Art direction and book design by Marijka Kostiw

FOR
MY FAMILY
— D.R.

TO
TWO SPECIAL FRIENDS:
KATHERINE MARINUCCI
— S.A.
&
WILLIAM DOUGLAS
— S.Q.

Snow fell in Rochester, New York.
A horse pulled a creaky buggy
down Madison Street.

Susan B. Anthony

set out two saucers,
two cups, and two slices of cake.

Frederick Douglass
arrived for tea.

Susan lit two candles on
the table.

The friends sat by the
fireplace in Susan's parlor.

Frederick wore a gentleman's
jacket, vest, and tie.

Susan wore a kind of pants called "bloomers."
She liked them better than the heavy dresses
women were supposed to wear.
Those dresses made it hard to get things done.

And Susan had many things to do.

As a girl, Susan wanted to learn what boys learned.

But teachers wouldn't let her.

Girls didn't need to know about important subjects, people said.
They should grow up to raise children, and that's all.

Susan's mother couldn't vote, or own a house, or go to college.

Few women could.

Susan wanted something more.
She read about rights in the United States.

The right to live free.
The right to vote.

Some people had rights, while others had none.

Why shouldn't she have them, too?

Susan taught herself to give speeches.

Some people liked her ideas about rights for women.

OUTRAGEOUS!

Others didn't.

The candles glowed in the parlor.
Frederick sipped his tea.
Susan asked him about his
newspaper.

He filled it with his own ideas
about rights.

is of no color

...... Truth is of no color ......

*"Everyone is talking about
my new issue!"* he said.

Frederick grew up as a slave in the South.
Slaves had to do everything the master said,
but Frederick wanted something more.
He secretly learned to read and write.

New ideas thrilled him.

Frederick read about rights in the United States.

The right to live free.
The right to vote.

Some people had rights, while others had none.

Why shouldn't he have them, too?

Frederick escaped from his master and headed north.
He taught himself to give speeches.
Some people liked his ideas about rights for African Americans.

Others didn't.

Susan liked Frederick's ideas,
and he liked hers.

He moved to Rochester and got
in touch with her.

They promised to help each other,
   so one day all people could have rights.

The fire crackled.
Snow fell outside the window.

Frederick and Susan ate their cake

and talked about their plans.

So many speeches to give.
So many articles to write.

So many minds to change.

They would get right to work.

As soon as they finished their tea.

Author's Note

This book imagines what it was like when Frederick Douglass met Susan B. Anthony at her house to talk about ideas. The two became friends in Rochester, New York, in the mid-1800s. At that time, slavery was legal in the United States, and so was discrimination against women. Anthony worked hard for women's rights, as did Douglass for African American rights. They made themselves into two of our greatest champions of freedom.

Anthony and Douglass both challenged unfair laws. Douglass escaped from slavery and also sheltered other runaway slaves in his house as part of the "Underground Railroad." Anthony voted in the 1872 election even though she knew the police would arrest her for it.

The two of them bravely spoke out for each other's causes, making appearances together throughout their lives. They never stopped fighting, and they never doubted that victory would come.

"Failure is impossible," Susan said.

Anthony and Douglass won their battles. The United States ended slavery in 1865 and gave women the right to vote in 1920.

Today, in Rochester, where they used to live, a statue shows the two friends having tea.

Bibliography

Barry, Kathleen. *Susan B. Anthony: A Biography of a Singular Feminist.* Bloomington, Indiana: First Books Library, 2000.

Davis, David Brion. *Inhuman Bondage: The Rise and Fall of Slavery in the New World.* New York: Oxford University Press, 2006.

Douglass, Frederick. *My Bondage and My Freedom.* Edited by John David Smith. New York: Penguin Classics, 2003.

Douglass, Frederick. *Narrative of the Life of Frederick Douglass, an American Slave.* New York: Sterling Publishing Company, 2003.

McFeely, William S. *Frederick Douglass.* New York: W.W. Norton & Company, 1991.

Sherr, Lynn. *Failure Is Impossible: Susan B. Anthony in Her Own Words.* New York: Times Books, 1996.

Ward, Geoffrey C., and Ken Burns. *Not for Ourselves Alone: The Story of Elizabeth Cady Stanton and Susan B. Anthony.* New York: Knopf, 1999.

Susan B. Anthony (1820–1906)

Frederick Douglass (1818–1895)